# For Mom & Dad
## (who taught me how to hug)

# A Book of Hugs

## by Dave Ross

## Thomas Y. Crowell    New York

LIBRARY OF CONGRESS CATALOGING IN PUBLICATION DATA
Ross, Dave. A book of hugs.
SUMMARY: Describes a variety of hugs, including people hugs, blanket hugs, and birthday hugs, and presents
facts and hints about hugs.
[1. Hugging—Fiction]  I.  Title. PZ7.R71964Bo      [E]      79-7896      ISBN 0-694-00146-5

hug (həg), *v.*, hugged, hug·ging
—*v.t.* 1. To clasp a person or thing in one's arms; to embrace [? Scand; cf. Icel *hugga* to soothe, console; akin to OE *hogian* to care for] — *n.* an embrace

hugger, *n.*, one who hugs [*see* A]—Ant., huggee [Obs.] a person or thing that receives a hug [*see* B]

huggable, adj., possessing an affectionate nature or qualities desirable to hug [*see* fig. 1]—Ant., unhuggable [*see* fig. 2]

figure 1

figure 2

# Animal Hugs
## Fish Hugs

Fish hugs are very cold and seldom returned.
P.S. Never hug a shark.

# Three kinds of Bear Hugs

(bare!)

Bear hugs are very strong. Be careful not to hurt.

# Octopus Hug

An octopus hugs with its whole body.

# Porcupine Hug

Porcupine hugs are done very carefully.

# Puppy Hugs

Puppy hugs are very soft and wet.

# Fraidycat Hugs

Fraidycat hugs make you feel safe.

# Piggyback Hug*

\* Sometimes called riding piggyback.

A good way to travel or see a parade.

# People Hugs
## Mommy Hugs

You can never hug a Mommy too much.

# Daddy Hug

Daddy hugs are best when he first walks in the door.

# Grandpa Hugs

Grandpa hugs are sometimes given while sitting.

# Grandma Hugs

Grandma hugs can be found anywhere, but
are especially nice in the kitchen.

# Brother Hug ✱
✱Usually called a Buddy Hug.

Note:
A circle of buddy huggers is called a huddle.

# Sister Hug✳

✳Also known as a Single-Arm Hug.

Single-arm hugs are good for people who walk together (even if they aren't sisters).

# BabyHugs

Baby hugs are given with a little tickle.
(Sometimes they can get you a little wet.)

# Great Aunt Mary Hug

A Great Aunt Mary hug can be given by any large lady you see only once a year. (You will usually end up with lipstick on your cheek.)

# ArmHugs

Arm hugs are good for people who are too big for you to get your arms around.

# Hand Hugs*

*Usually called holding hands.
Sometimes called shaking hands.

Never hand-hug with dirty hands unless the other person has dirty hands too.

# Knee Hugs

Knee hugs are for tall people.
Warning: Never try to knee-hug a moving person.

# Thing Hugs
## Blanket Hug

**Everyone needs some kind of blanket.**

# Tree Hugs

Some trees are easier to hug than others.
Note: If you hug a pine tree too long you get stuck on it.

# Rock Hugs

BE A LITTLE BOULDER

Rock hugs are very hard on your face.

# Pricker Bush Hugs

Never hug a pricker bush. (Or poison ivy or cactus.)

# Ice Cube Hug

Ice cube hugs are quite common in February.

# Lamppost Hug

A lamppost hug can save you from a painful experience.

# Sandwich Hug

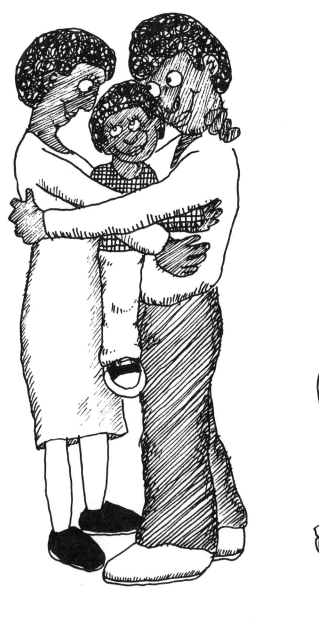

The whole family can get into a sandwich hug.

# Special Hugs
## Birthday Hugs

A birthday hug is a present anyone can afford.

# Report Card Hugs

**A Hug**

**Bee Hug**

**Sea Hug**

# Hurt Hugs

Hurt hugs make the pain go away.

# Winner Hugs

# Loser Hugs

# Facts & Hints About Hugs

There is no such thing as a bad hug:
there are only good hugs and great hugs.

Hug someone at least once a day and
twice on a rainy day.

Hug with a smile; closed eyes are optional.

A snuggle is a longish hug.

Bedtime hugs help chase away bad dreams

Never hug tomorrow someone you could
hug today.